The KING'S TETHER

A Chained Gods Series Prequel Story

Tamira Thayne

Published by Who Chains You Publishing
P.O. Box 581
Amissville, VA 20106
www.WhoChainsYou.com

Design and layout by Tamira Thayne

ISBN-13: 978-1-946044-09-9
ISBN-10: 1-946044-09-1

Printed in the United States of America

First Edition

❦

In Memory of my shepherd, Sloan
who spent his life on a chain
before his rescue.

You were a King to me, boy.

Also by Tamira Thayne

AUTHOR OF
The King's Tether:
A Chained Gods Series Prequel Story

The Wrath of Dog:
The Chained Gods Series Book 1

The Curse of Cur:
The Chained Gods Series Book 2

Foster Doggie Insanity:
Tips and Tales to Keep your Kool as a Doggie Foster Parent

Capitol in Chains: 54 Days of the Doghouse Blues

Smidgey Pidgey's Predicament

Raffy Calfy's Rescue

Happy Dog Coloring Book: From Chained to Cherished

EDITOR OF
Rescue Smiles: Favorite Animal Stories
of Love and Liberation

More Rescue Smiles: Beloved Animal Tales
of Freedom and Devotion

Unchain My Heart: Dogs Deserve Better Rescue
Stories of Courage, Compassion, and Caring

Contents

Inspiration for The King, photo courtesy Darin Ashby, dashdezigns.com.
Unfortunately, dogs all over the world still live this way today.

Dreams

In a rare moment of inactivity, the dog rested his head on his front paws. The thick logging chain weighed heavily across his body as he pulled his back legs from beneath the oppressive steel.

He was too depleted to keep up the heavy pacing, too thirsty to pant, too hungry to lift his nose to the air in search of food.

On the infrequent occasion he caught the scent of prey, the links of rusted metal kept his skeletal form from achieving his goal.

He was slated to remain in perpetual starvation and dehydration.

Yet he could not die.

His eyelids drooped, and though his feral mind urged him to remain vigilant, told him he was in constant danger, sleep had its way with him anyway.

With sleep came relief.

In the waking state his mind knew only bloodlust and revenge, his body hunger and thirst, and his heart pain and sorrow. In slumber his consciousness freed itself from the falsely implanted bonds, and he revisited a life once known—only to lose the beloved memories upon reawakening.

The ultimate cruelty.

In the dream he searched for a woman. It couldn't be just any woman; according to the Prophetess, he would know her when he saw her.

After months of scouting, his despair had grown at the impossibility of the task. No woman drew him to her, there was no siren's call. He and his team of adept men and women had scoured the country, the world, yet there'd been no pull. Anywhere.

In frustration he'd bid his squad to remain behind today. He needed to clear his head, logging the 30 miles to the peaks of the Shenandoah Mountains alone in order to lose himself in the beauty Earth offered through the breathtaking vistas of Skyline Drive.

He rarely transformed himself to his canine form since coming here, because the search for the woman had been all-consuming; there was simply no time allotted for fun or relaxation, the gift of peace offered by his shepherd counterpart.

But he would quickly reach the point of explosion if he didn't release some of this pent-up anxiety. The future of his dimension rested on his weary shoulders, and the lack of progress toward his end-goal was beyond frustrating.

Spotting a pull-off with signs for the Appalachian Trail,

he made a snap decision. Yanking the steering wheel to the right, he smoothly cruised the old Jaguar into the nearest parking spot. He smiled to himself at the mental image of a dog driving a car with a cat emblem perched on the hood. Only he was aware of the irony, and it was one of his little inside jokes that, truth be told, had a lot to do with his choice in vehicle.

He locked up and hiked a few hundred yards up the trail before ducking behind a tree and disrobing. In dog form he had no need for clothing, but he'd definitely require his skivvies and other trappings to return to his car as a human.

He hid his clothes and keys beneath a mountain laurel bush, and quickly and painlessly transformed himself into his German shepherd—happier—half. He broke away from the marked trail to save himself any interactions with humans who might peg him for a lost dog, picked up a deer trail, and sprinted full on through the mountains.

Heaven's Gate! This was exactly what he needed to discharge some of that tension. After his wildly-freeing initial release, he slowed down, loping and sniffing his way for well over two hours before tiring and turning reluctantly back toward the trail, his clothing, his car, and the resumption of his search.

It was dusk when he finally reached his Jag and backed out of the spot. As he cruised toward the lot's exit, a woman stumbled from the woods and collapsed face first 20 feet in front of his car. He screeched to a halt, shock firing an all-cylinders adrenaline rush.

But there was something more. Every cell in his body reached for her before he'd thought to even exit the auto. His brain, his heart, his mind—they all called to her, whispering of bonds and mating rituals and a shared future that was theirs and theirs alone.

A kick to the ribs lurched him from the dream, and the woman slipped away from him, again.

Dog Abuse

His feral mind was relentless in its urge to kill, maim, exact vengeance on these beings who dare imprison him. He was trapped not only by the physical presence of the chain, but also by a malevolent, lurking cloud in his own psyche that pushed him above and beyond the paranoia of a true feral dog. There were no higher or rational reasoning skills that he could depend on to get him out of this predicament.

His everyday existence was fraught with ceaseless anger, pain, bloodlust, and abuse and neglect at the hands of his captors.

The kick came again, only this time he was awake, ready for it. He pivoted and threw himself in the direction of his tormentor, lashing out with wide mouth and massive canines. He reached the end of his chain and was yanked cruelly back by a tether with no give, his body flung to the side as his head was whipped to the rear.

The man's laugh taunted his prisoner as he skipped out of range and carelessly tossed down some leftovers…just out of reach of the dog's chain.

But even as starved as the feral was, his mind remained focused on the man, ignoring the food—he could always come back for that later. For now he wanted a piece of the man in black, and he wanted it bad. Saliva dripped from his mouth.

Adrenaline pumping through his system, his flight or fight response kicked into overdrive by the continued presence of his abductor. He knew this scent. Without access to higher reasoning, he relied on instinct and smell; smell told him the man was one of those who regularly tormented him and instinct told him to lure the human into the bounds created by the chain.

He dragged himself as if gravely injured toward the ramshackle doghouse which acted as his sole means of shelter. Ignoring the man, he crawled to the opening and flopped down in front of it, favoring the side where he'd been kicked. He closed his eyes, giving the illusion of overwhelming pain, which wasn't far from the truth.

The man cursed and yelled at him, but picked up a few pieces of the food and threw them closer to where he lay. When the dog make no move to go after the scraps, the man hesitated, less concerned about the dog's passing than his own skin if he ended up dead on his watch.

He crept to the dog's empty pan, lugging a plastic jug of dirty water, and filled the bowl while keeping one eye on the shepherd. His fatal mistake came in looking down to ensure he'd hit his mark. The dog lunged, grabbing him by the throat and shaking him as if he were a groundhog. He growled fiercely, biting, shredding.

The shepherd dredged up a fearsome strength, silencing the man's screams in just a few breaths and standing over him with his lip curled while the last of the man's lifeblood gurgled from his throat into the parched soil.

He felt no remorse, no happiness, no guilt. Only a vague sense of satisfaction at making this one less captor who would ever torment him again.

Too bad there were others.

He calmly walked over to the rations the man had thrown his way, devouring every dirt-covered morsel, and then ambled to the water dish. It hadn't spilled in the man's death throes, and he drank almost his fill for the first time in months.

He sat and waited for the man's friends to arrive, wondering if he could add them to his collection of dead men. He would not have long to wait.

PUNISHMENT

More men in black soon appeared, shouting and cursing in a repeat of the last man's actions before his untimely demise. But this time there were three of them, and he knew his chances were greatly diminished. The first two moved to distract the dog, plunging into his territory and zipping away before he could latch onto them, while the third dragged the body to safety.

These men were fast. Faster than he'd remembered, so fast he couldn't follow their movements. He felt even more confused than usual, unable to keep up with them, and the 50-lb. anchor he dragged did him no favors.

They carried devices which they used to lash out at him, the force slamming him in the chest, stopping his forward momentum—and nearly stopping his heart, too. He blew backward and crashed into the doghouse, the wind and every scrap of strength he'd obtained from the food and water depleted from his body.

He struggled to stand again, to fight, but he was engulfed by a burning pain. He felt defeated, his injuries much more dire this time than the last.

These men were not as gullible as the former, and blasted him again, pushing him just shy of the point of death. They left him there, bleeding and broken, their laughter lingering as they disappeared, bragging that he would never mess with one of their own again.

Blissful oblivion overcame him, and he tumbled into the dreamworld.

FIGHT

The challenge for his dimension's throne was a three-day event for participants and a non-stop party for the spectators. He'd thought long, trained hard, but still felt unprepared, tremulous, when the time came to call out the king. Egged on by his warriors, he'd pushed his fear aside and set the terms of the challenge.

The king's acceptance came by messenger within hours.

Three days. Five matches. One winner—with a kingdom, the future path of a dimension, at stake.

The first two days were devoted solely to head games and mental competitions, sparking a heated rivalry as edginess and testosterone built between the two men; it was well-known amongst both contenders and Perrin's citizens that whoever came out on top in the initial bouts still had to prove himself in the arena, and the energy swelled toward the final battle's release.

When they fought, each would bring eight warriors onto the field with him, and winners were judged on leadership and the ability to show compassion for one's enemies in addition to combat readiness.

On his dimension, this more-enlightened contest signified a society that had evolved beyond the days of old, the days when raw greed overpowered ethics to seize control. The overtly power-hungry were no longer tolerated, and when necessary the people stood as one to ensure those with control used it wisely. The people of Perrin expected strength of character tempered with kindness and purpose from their leaders.

He had rather easily bested the king in most of the mind games, his prowess and command of his mental gifts were not over-exaggerated; this piqued a stir of whispered murmurings amongst the people, unease coupled with excitation at the possibility of an unknown future.

He'd overtaken King Terrence in three of four challenges, the exception being historical facts and knowledge of the inner workings of the kingdom. Terrence had been on the throne for 850 years—there was nothing about this dimension and the law that he didn't know and understand. It showed.

But here, now, in this battle, he had his chance as the challenger to put it away, to clutch that for which he'd trained over the past two centuries. He knew the fight would be difficult. His team was ready, they'd been drilling for this their entire lives, but that didn't make it any easier. He had to ensure he came out on top, but also that his warriors came through safely too.

The arena was packed with Perrinite citizens, screaming and yelling both his name and the name of the king. The people seemed divided on who they wanted to win, and he felt a flash of amazement at how quickly even the supposedly enlightened succumbed to bloodlust.

6

The king circled him, spittle lingering at the edges of his mouth. Their warriors engaged each other in separate conflicts all around them, but the rules stated no one interfered with the king and his challenger without being specifically drawn into the conflict by one of the two. He'd instructed his team to hold off unless Terrence crossed that line first, to best the other warriors if possible, but without doing any lasting harm. They'd acquiesced.

He stumbled, suddenly wondered why he was doing this. He knew King Terrence was a good man. One of the best, in fact, and he had considered him a friend.

But, even though in this dimension men didn't physically age past their prime if they didn't choose it, after 1000 years a certain torpor still showed in a man's eyes. Leaders became stuck in their own ways, the old ways of thinking. They stopped being open to new ideas and new paths for the country, and that's what Perrin currently faced.

They had stagnated, and everyone knew it.

It was time for new blood, a new direction. His resolve strengthened, and he took on the contest with renewed fervor. Friend or foe, Terrence had to go.

Terrence was no slouch in the ring and, as king, had faced more than his fair share of challengers over the past eight centuries. There were no weapons allowed; they fought with their hands and whatever wits they brought into the arena with them. Their mental powers, which had been tested every which way over the past two days, were prohibited in this last match; anyone caught using them would forfeit the fight and their shot at ruling the kingdom.

Terrence moved to the right, predicting the challenger's next move. But he'd guessed wrong, his contender faking right and then sweeping his feet out from under him. The king fell heavily, but rolled backward and sprung up, evading the kick headed his way. They circled each other, in truth both loath to do physical harm and finding no way around it.

The audience grumbled, quickly growing disenchanted.

This was the problem with men of honor—they had a distaste for inflicting harm.

The challenger lunged again, this time connecting with Terrence's ribs, and the snap of bone and inadvertent *oof* of pain could be heard all the way to the stands. People cheered or booed according to their preferences, and both men grappled for the upper hand.

The fight would have been considered boring by any standards.

Three hours later the men stood, arms around each other to prevent sucker punches, more exhausted than injured. Neither was ready to give up, both convinced he was the better man to lead his people.

The contender knew if he didn't take decisive action soon he would lose by default. His team had quickly and impressively subdued the king's warriors without inflicting grave injury, making him the weak link. It was time to stop letting his conscience hold him back…he knew he'd been waffling because he didn't want to harm the king. It went against every ounce of loyalty ingrained in him.

Yes, he respected the king; yes, he felt like a traitor for challenging him, but he'd been led by an inner knowing that he was on the right path. He held firm to the truth of this belief deep in his gut, yet he'd been allowing his feelings to stand in the way. It was time to end this.

He pushed off from the hold position and quickly followed with an upper cut to Terrence's jaw. Two more immediate hits followed to already-tender ribs, and when the king doubled over, he leapt from behind and ended it, choking him out until he fell unconscious.

Terrence didn't get up this time.

The fight had finally finished.

The new king only wished he felt good about it.

He stood, hoisted aloft by his warriors, and raised his arms in victory. He resolved to lead his people into a new and brighter future. The cheering of the crowd resounded in his ears like an ill omen, for they confirmed just how fickle were those he now led.

Familiar

The dog awoke to a blanket of pain coating his body. If it weren't for the scraps of food and water he'd ingested earlier, he wondered if he'd have woken at all. There wasn't a location on his body that didn't hurt, throb, or bleed.

He dragged himself to the water bowl desperate for one more drop, but it was bone dry. He looked to the sky in hopes of rain, but those hopes were quickly dashed, too.

Most of his thirst was quenched solely from the puddles within reach of his chain—dirty water caught in the holes he dug from boredom and frustration.

He urged himself to begin the pacing ritual that signaled to his brain and body that he was still alive. He paced in the circle dictated by chain length, along the worn path his paws had wrought in years-long feverish yet futile activity. There was little grass left on which to lay his head, most ripped out by the chain as it dragged across the tender shoots brave enough to stick their heads above ground. His home was packed dirt and piles of his own defecation, which he instinctively attempted to confine to a single area far from his decrepit house.

On this morning, like so many of the past few years, a young human skirted his area on her way to school. He terrified her, and it gave him some small satisfaction to do so, triggering the thrill of the hunt. He smelled her fear, but there was something else about her scent, too. Something familiar, like he should know her. His senses pinged when she drew near, and somewhere within the fog of his mind he reached for something long forgotten.

He was less inclined toward a murderous rampage with her than others passing by, but his feral mind didn't register much past a general feeling of confusion as to why. This ambivalence never stopped him from lashing out at her each morning, reveling in her terror and fear, as if in creating it within her he could ease the throb of his own torment.

Some mornings she tossed him a biscuit as she scurried by, more to distract him than anything else, but he was happy to have it, momentarily forgetting his bullying in a rush to stave off starvation.

This morning he wasn't able to climb to his feet long enough to torture her; his wounds prevented him from doing the very job he'd been placed there to do.

He watched her walk by, her eyes widening in fear and concern, and then slumped back to the ground by his dog-house. Oblivion claimed him once again.

A King

Born in Earth year 997 A.D., the man had by now surpassed his 1000th birthday, if such things were measured on his dimension. He held to the appearance of a twenty-something, his dark good looks, angular face, and well-manicured hair putting one in mind of his shepherd counterpart.

It had taken him fully 200 years to develop his powers and prove himself the strongest immortal on the planet, taking over as king after besting his predecessor in a three-day contest those many moons ago. Many had challenged him and lost since those early days, and he incessantly trained both himself and his team in order to keep them geared up for the next contender.

The unceasing power grabs and the ever-present threat of control falling into the wrong hands weighed heavily on his mind, especially after ruling Perrin for 800 years, give or take. He couldn't help but question if by now he, like Terrence before him, had fallen prey to tunnel vision; was it time for him to step aside and allow new blood to invigorate the land?

But what if his people suffered as a result? What if they were taken over by the lurking evil he felt waiting for an opportunity to wend its way into the seat of power?

He'd become king early in the 13th century, and had been undermined by those of ill-intentioned ilk ever since. One dissenter, Phoebus, had even gone so far as to impregnate an Earthen woman, engendering a line of hybrids that was prophesied to destroy his dimension, his people, his very way of life.

In a necessarily decisive move, the king put forth a decree that no citizen of Perrin was authorized to visit Earth after Phoebus' deception was discovered. A curse was put onto anyone violating the law by his sorceress, Mara, ensuring that anyone who copulated with a human would lose not only the right to return to Perrin but so much more.

When the first mixed child to carry the blood of a Perrinite proved to possess just a slightly longer life span than the average human, all breathed a sigh of relief, hoping the line would eventually die out on its own, freeing them from the terrifying prophecy.

Unfortunately, it hadn't happened, and as a result they faced the ultimate destruction of all he and his people held dear.

He'd always believed he would willingly die for his people, his province, and now it seemed he would be called upon to test this readiness. Would it all be worth it? Would they be saved in the end, even as he sacrificed himself?

If all went as planned, the irony was that he'd never know the outcome. Regardless, he steadfastly prepared himself and his team to visit earth in search of their salvation.

But not his own, alas. There would be no salvation for him.

GIRL

The girl was back, but this time she wasn't alone. There was a woman with her, a woman whose smell also teased his senses. He backed up, confusion sending alarm signals to his fuzzy brain. Who were these people?

They stood back and assessed him, and although he had regained some small measure of physical health, he still didn't feel well enough to be his normal threatening self.

They were leery, watching him, waiting. Neither wanted to approach, and for good reason. They were smart enough not to trust him, probably smarter than those arrogant men in black.

He remembered seeing the woman drive by many times, and she'd sometimes thrown food from her car to the ground within his reach, but he'd never caught such a powerful whiff of her before.

What was it...

He briefly wished that he could remember, but his mind was so far gone that the presence of two people he wasn't set on killing was enough to throw off his day.

The woman started to walk toward him, slowly, and he growled, standing his ground. He wasn't about to start trusting anyone, especially a human, not now. Not ever.

He backed up to the length of his chain, head down, tail flagged, and stared her dead in the eye. She received the message, immediately reversing course and standing uncertainly next to the girl again.

Food, water, idiots—he would have said if he were capable of human speech. Instead, the mental images of these basic needs floated through his mind, and he pushed them forcefully toward the women.

They hurried off together up the alley and were back in ten minutes, arms laden with food and water. They tossed dry kibble and a can of dog chow onto the ground off to his right; when he dashed over to gulp the now dust-covered banquet they veered left to fill his water bowl.

Clean water!

He'd missed it, ached for it, and had he been an average dog, would have died long ago without it. If there was ever a moment he could weep since his feral transformation, this would have been that moment. The men who occasionally brought him food and water tarnished everything they touched with the taste and smell of dirt to assert their dominance over him.

Their callousness over his treatment had quickly turned a feral dog into one with a deadly mission and a sole focus. Revenge.

These women would never be able to change that.

He left off eating and dove for the water bowl, burying his nose in the clean, cool liquid, slurping until every last drop had seeped into his skeletal frame. Then he licked the bowl just in case. He appreciated the food and water—to the extent that he was capable of, at least. He had basic needs like all living beings, and given that they had just met the two most essential without causing him further injury made him a tad less mistrustful of them.

Maybe they would keep bringing it...and if they did, he would try very hard not to kill them.

It was the best he could do.

They watched him devour his food and water, conferred together, then left and returned again with treats and another gallon of water; this time, his belly actually felt overfull for the first time in his memory, not that that was saying much.

With the nutrition jump-starting his healing abilities, his wounds slowly began to knit together, pushing out the infection and renewing his strength. The sun made an appearance, and he lay in its warmth and dozed, the closest he'd come to contentment since his kidnapping eighteen years ago.

UNEXPECTED

He doubled over, clutching his sides, not from pain, but from an unexpected source: laughter. He and the woman rolled off the bed and onto the floor, she on top of him tickling for all she was worth.

What is this thing she called tickling? Why did it hurt so unbearably yet cause him to howl with glee at the same time? He couldn't believe the little things she was teaching him about his human form, little things that he hadn't learned in 1000 years on his dimension.

He shrieked and tried to get away from her, but she clung like a burr, crying she was laughing so hard at his dilemma. As it turned out, he was ticklish everywhere…including his feet, his ribs, his armpits, his stomach. Even the back of his neck!

She was a witch!

He finally got her off and streaked through the house, running like a man with his pants on fire. She shadowed him, a stalking beast, having no idea how fast he could actually be if he turned on the juice, or that he was allowing her to catch him.

As she turned the corner, he grabbed her up in his arms and swung her, high from laughter and the feel of her against him. The mirth died as he set her down, pushing her chocolate hair back from her face.

His eyes caught and held hers.

He was in love, for the first time in his life, and he couldn't believe how decadent it felt…how unimaginably delightful! He slowly lowered his head and gently pecked her lips… then a little less gently…and soon their ardor had ignited, turning their kisses urgent and their hands fervid.

Lifting her slender form, he carried her to the bedroom, to the place of his tickle torture, laying her atop the rumpled sheets. What little they were wearing soon slipped off…he was convinced no one else on the planet made love as passionately as they did, or felt as deliciously expended afterward.

They cuddled in tight, not able to get close enough to one another, and she fell asleep to the rise and fall of his chest. He watched the sun peek over the windowsill, and wondered where things went from here.

He was captivated, enamored, but he also carried the heaviness of a secret, his burden, his reason for seeking her out: he needed her with child, and he needed it sooner rather than later.

But how does one ask such a thing of the woman he loves? How does one tell his paramour that he is using her to produce an offspring slated to go to war for his people?

In no possible scenario did that admission end well for him.

As he lay there, deep in thought, a seed of hope took root within his chest. Maybe, just maybe, the curse wouldn't take; maybe he could stay here with her, maybe they could raise a family together, and face all that ugly when it reared its ferocious head.

For the first time in his life, the idea of a home and family not only mattered to him, it consumed him.

Sameness

The feral's physical health improved over the next weeks, thanks to the nourishment provided by the females and his immortality, which brought him back from the brink of death time and again. His mental state would remain unchanged, and he paced his circle for hours in an attempt to release some of the twisted hatred coiled about his spine.

All was quiet for the time being with his tormenters. They were withholding food and water in an attempt to punish him for slaying one of their own, not knowing he'd been cared for by local good samaritans. Without the sustenance provided by the girl and the woman, his suffering would have been immeasurable.

The girl often threw him a biscuit on her way to school. He menaced her, especially on the days she forgot, in an effort to ensure she brought him more biscuits.

She forgot less often now.

About once a week she and the other woman would show up with kibble and water, toss the food to the right, and duck left to fill his water dish while he gobbled every crumb. They had no way of knowing that was the only food and water he got all week…they incorrectly assumed they were supplementing a meager diet, having no understanding of the depravity of his captors.

He paced to his crumbling house and flopped in front of it. Bored, he gnawed on a rotten piece of wood that was sticking out the side, yanking it clear of the debris and holding it between his paws. The house was so tumble-down that the idea of it providing any means of shelter was unthinkable.

He chewed detachedly, swallowing the wood chunks as if it were a meal, both hungry and apathetic to any damage it could cause. After all, even if the splinters perforated his intestines, his immortality would probably find a way to patch him back up again.

His thoughts, if it could be said that he had any, remained muddled and murky. Since the advent of the girl they had become a little less threatening, were he able to reason them out, but bloodlust and revenge still dominated his demeanor.

He was snared in a life he had no desire to live, and he could find no way out. He would have sooner died, but his immortality was as much of a trap as the chain.

The anger festered, and it was directed at the men who enmeshed him in this hell. The men in black. Each man looked much like the next, covered in black from head to toe: black shirts, black pants, black shoes. He differentiated them solely by their scent and the tenor of their voices.

If he could put words to mental images, the closest he would have come to describing them would have been ninjas.

But, where did they come from, and why had they put him here?

He couldn't think clearly enough to begin to ponder the answers to these questions.

Baby

She was with child!

I'm going to be a father. He sat heavily back onto the sofa, his mind whirling at a frenetic pace. Hope, happiness, shame, sadness, all were at war within his soul.

He'd accomplished his mission to Earth, but at what price for himself, his lover, his child. Exactly how much would each have to give, how much would be left for them as a family when they were done sacrificing for his dimension?

These were questions seemingly without answers, but the pain wound itself around his heart and started a gentle squeeze.

There would be no easy way out of this problem.

For them, there was only through.

PACK

The pack had never felt such relief, their joy swelling and reverberating throughout the bonds, collectively blissing them all out. It was like they'd taken community happy pills.

They'd actually found her—the woman they'd sought for almost a year of their lives, the woman who would help them fulfill the prophecy. They'd discovered the golden needle in an entire meadow of haystacks.

Things with her had progressed beyond what he'd ever dreamed imaginable, and perhaps it was the high of his feelings for her that had become the happy pill creating euphoria amongst the pack. He'd take it. If he could bottle this emotion to seal within his soul for the rest of eternity, he'd do it in a heartbeat.

In truth, the king didn't understand why he hadn't yet suffered the consequences of flouting his own law—why he'd not yet turned feral, forgotten his pack, his love, his immortal form, and duties as their leader. That's what was supposed to happen, according to the curse, the curse he'd devised with the help of the Sorceress.

He shoved the thought down to the dungeons of his mind.

This was a time for celebration, reveling in the moment,

and not a time for self-pity or wasted concern about an uncertain future.

He pulled his mind back to the eight men and women surrounding him. His team hadn't been able to run as a pack since they'd arrived on earth over a year and a half ago, and they were chomping at the bit to get going, experience the mental and physical release of their dog forms.

Today was *their* day, and he would not take that happiness from them.

They piled into two large SUVs for the trip to the Shenandoah Mountains, parking in the same lot where he'd found the woman—his good-luck spot. He led his team to the patch of mountain laurel where he'd hidden his clothes that first time, hastily scouting the area to assure himself there were no human or other prying eyes about.

Satisfied, they began the transformation into their dog counterparts, some able to change quickly and others taking longer, depending on their particular gifts. The king patiently awaited his warriors, excited to lead them on the day's chase through the rocky terrain.

One by one they proudly stood as canines, quivering in an effort to contain their excitement: two more shepherds, an Akita, three retrievers, and two St. Bernards. They were a majestic group, the elite of the Perrin guard.

When finished, the king linked into their minds, giving the signal to begin the chase. He steered them along the ridges of the mountains, where they gleefully herded deer, a bobcat, and even a bear, who wisely chose to tree himself and wait for their exuberance to pass.

As they ran, the pack dropped away the concerns of their human lives and drew in the contentment that came with lessening those day-to-day apprehensions and living in the moment.

He wasn't sure exactly when it occurred, but suddenly those mundane cares slipped even further, along with his memories of the woman and the life they were building together.

He felt a brief moment of panic, realizing his worst fears were coming true, and there was nothing he could do to stop it. *No!*

His soul cried out for her. His reason for living was being stolen from him, along with every memory of his immortal life, Perrin, Earth, and his soon-to-be-born child.

Through his link to the minds of his pack he felt them as they slipped away, too, grasping at the straws of their lives as they passed them by.

Soon the king and his team of elite warriors were nothing more than they appeared on the surface: a pack of wild dogs who made the mountains their home.

Whereas earlier they'd chased animals without intention of doing harm, now they would survive off these same animals, kill them for food, find a den for housing.

An inborn instinct led him and his packmates to a cave system along a rocky outcropping at the base of the mountains. It would do.

They lived those next months simply, joyfully, as ferals, having no memory of ever being more.

Until the day they were captured by men in black.

Hope

The dog awoke to the sound of birds chirping and the not unpleasant breeze of a late fall morning. He stretched, feeling physically better than he had in a long, long time. He gnawed at his leg, trying to rid himself of the fleas taking their share of his recent bounty. He scratched behind his ear, where a stubborn tick and her newborns were reluctant to move onto greener pastures.

He stood, stretched into downward facing dog, and then reversed into upward facing dog. He lazily paced the circle of his yard, but his pace was lest frenetic than just yesterday. He tried once again and in vain to get past the fog in his mind, but to no avail.

He paced, scratched, bit; paced, scratched, bit.

He waited, looking for the girl or the woman who brought him food and water. No one.

He paced, scratched, bit; paced, scratched, bit.

Finally, he again lay down, his head on his paws. As he drifted off to sleep, he felt something he never remembered feeling before.

Hope.

He didn't know why, but he sensed that maybe something better was on the horizon. Maybe it was.

We hope you enjoyed Tamira Thayne's
*The King's Tether: A Chained Gods Series
Prequel Story.* This story precedes
The Wrath of Dog, and can be read before *Book 1*
or after to flesh out the character of the King.

COULD YOU TAKE A MOMENT TO GIVE THE STORY
A SHORT REVIEW ON AMAZON.COM? YOUR REVIEWS
MEAN THE WORLD TO OUR AUTHORS, AND HELP THEM
EXPAND THEIR AUDIENCE AND THEIR VOICE.
THANK YOU SO MUCH!

Find links to The King's Tether, The Wrath of Dog,
*and all our great books
on Amazon or at www.whochainsyou.com.*

About the Author

Tamira Thayne pioneered the anti-tethering movement in America, forming and leading the nonprofit Dogs Deserve Better for 13 years.

During her time on the front lines of animal activism and rescue she took on plenty of bad guys (often failing miserably); her swan song culminated in the purchase and transformation of Michael Vick's dogfighting compound to a chained-dog rescue and rehabilitation center. She's spent 878 hours chained to a doghouse on behalf of the voiceless in front of state capitol buildings nationwide, and worked with her daughter to take on a school system's cat dissection program, garnering over 100,000 signatures against the practice.

She's the author of *The Knight's Chain, The King's Tether, The Wrath of Dog, The Cur of Cur, Foster Doggie Insanity, Smidgey Pidgey's Predicament, Spittin' Kitten's Speed-Away, Raffy Calfy's Rescue,* and *Capitol in Chains.* She's the editor of *More Rescue Smiles,* and the co-editor of *Unchain My Heart* and *Rescue Smiles.*

In 2016 she founded Who Chains You, publishing books by and for animal activists and rescuers.

The Chained Gods Series Book 1

Excerpt from

THE WRATH OF DOG: THE CHAINED DOGS SERIES BOOK 1

The hairy beast growled and lunged at me, his rusted logging chain straining to break—like it did every morning I cut down his back alley.

"I need to find another way to school," I grumbled to myself, heart pounding as I looked away and shuffled past him. No reason to deliberately provoke the Wrath of Dog, my oh-so-aptly-dubbed title for him.

Truth be told, I pitied the thing. "What kind of asshat chains their dog outside?" I furthered my inner rant.

At the age of 17 (and a half, thank you very much) I already had a heart for the animals, a trait pounded into my head by my bleeding heart mother from the time I could walk.

I could go on and on about dogs and chaining, Mom's monologue was just that stuck in my brain. "Dogs deserve better than life on a chain," she'd fume and fuss each time we passed a dog like Wrath.

Yeah, Mom, I get it. Someday I'll free Wrath and we'll rise up and smite his nasty-ass owner. For today, though, I just need to get past him without dying and make it the two blocks to class before the bell rings and I have another detention headed my way.

Sometimes it sucked to be me.

But never as much as it sucks to be Wrath, my do-gooder conscience—sounding suspiciously like my mother—reminded me.

Gah. Where was a dog biscuit when you needed one?

With one last glance to make sure the chain was holding, I took off at a run through the remnants of yesterday's skiff of snow and up to the doors of the high school.

Wrath's plight was soon forgotten.

"Bay!" the cheery scream echoed down the corridor. I cringed, my introvert soul longing to slink away unnoticed. But my Leo best friend would have none of that as long as she was still kickin', above ground, and had any air left in her lungs to bellow.

My exact opposite in every way, Amaya was short to my tall, loud to my quiet, and blond to my brunette.

She was curvaceous, cute, and sassy, whereas I was willowy and somber, with more of a girl-next-door thing going for me. Lucky me.

We shared a love of snark, all things fur-covered, and a devotion to each other that went beyond the high-school best friendships that were here one day, gone the next.

I did adore her.

But maybe not today. Today I wanted to turn and flee as all eyes in the crowded pre-first-period hallway swept my way....

Read more and order from whochainsyou.com, Amazon, and other outlets.

Also from Tamira Thayne

FOSTER DOGGIE INSANITY: TIPS AND TALES TO KEEP YOUR KOOL AS A DOGGIE FOSTER PARENT

Have you ever fostered a dog—happy to make a difference—but wondered why you felt frustrated and alone in your experience? Do you want to foster a dog, but don't know where to start, how to prepare, and what to expect? Have you experienced burnout or compassion fatigue in your rescue experience? If so, this is the book for you. Described as "an embrace from a friend who understands what we all go through; it is a beacon of hope to let other rescuers know they are not alone—a must-read for anyone involved in rescue."

This is not a book about dog training, but a book about people training while working with dogs...*Read more and order from whochainsyou.com, Amazon, and other outlets.*

Also from Tamira Thayne

CAPITOL IN CHAINS:
54 DAYS OF THE DOGHOUSE BLUES

In August 2010, one woman carried a doghouse to the steps of the Pennsylvania State Capitol building and chained herself to it, seeking passage of a law protecting dogs from life at the end of a chain.

Not knowing if she'd be arrested, ignored, or ridiculed, she set aside her fears and acted on behalf of the voiceless: dogs—the most social of beings—whose needs have been overlooked by those with the power to create chain-ge for their future.

This is her story, and the story of the 54 days she and others spent chained at the bottom of the Capitol steps in Harrisburg, Pennsylvania. May you be inspired, entertained, and educated about the needs of Man's Best Friend, and how these needs continue to be negated in today's society....*Read more and order from whochainsyou.com, Amazon, and other outlets.*

www.ingramcontent.com/pod-product-compliance
Lightning Source LLC
Chambersburg PA
CBHW071225130626
46555CB00004B/1844